# Little Olympians

BOOK 3

## HERMES, THE
## FASTEST GOD

 little bee books

New York, NY
Copyright © 2021 by Little Bee Books
All rights reserved, including the right of reproduction in whole or in part in any form.
Manufactured in China  RRD 0621
littlebeebooks.com

Library of Congress Cataloging-in-Publication Data is available upon request.
ISBN: 978-1-4998-1153-7 (hc)
First Edition 10  9  8  7  6  5  4  3  2  1
ISBN: 978-1-4998-1154-4 (pbk)
First Edition 10  9  8  7  6  5  4  3  2  1
ISBN: 978-1-4998-1237-4 (ebook)

For information about special discounts on bulk purchases, please contact Little Bee Books at sales@littlebeebooks.com.

# HERMES, THE FASTEST GOD

BY A.I. NEWTON          ILLUSTRATED BY ANJAN SARKAR

little bee books

# TABLE OF CONTENTS

# THE GODS OF OLYMPUS

Once, all-powerful gods ruled from their home atop the cloud-covered heights of Mount Olympus: Zeus, God of Thunder; Athena, Goddess of Wisdom; Apollo, the Sun God; Ares, God of Combat; Aphrodite, Goddess of Beauty and Nature; Poseidon, God of the Seas, and others possessed incredible powers, and controlled the fate of humans on Earth . . .

1

. . . but these powerful beings were not always the mighty Gods of Olympus. Once, long ago, they were just a bunch of kids. . . .

# CHAPTER 1

# AN EXCITING JOURNEY

Hermes could not have been more excited. He and his fellow young gods were about to go on their first field trip since arriving at Eureka. He climbed into a golden carriage alongside Zeus, Athena, Apollo, Ares, Aphrodite, and Artemis. Beside them sat Poseidon. He was their counselor and also Zeus's big brother.

He tightly held reins that were attached
to a team of six flying horses, led by
Pegasus. At a command from Poseidon,
the horses leapt from the ground, spread
their mighty wings, and lifted the golden
carriage high into the sky above Eureka.

"Welcome to your first field trip," Poseidon said. "We are going to the city of Argos in Greece. There, you will get your first glimpse at the humans whose fate you will control once you have grown up, fully realized your powers, and taken your place alongside the other gods of Mount Olympus.

"This trip will help you see that your powers exist for a reason," Poseidon explained as they soared through the clouds. "They are only important if they can be used to help the mortals who live around us. And so, the time has come for you to observe them up close."

"Cool!" said Zeus, lightning crackling from his fingertips. "Wait until these humans get a load of my lightning and thunder."

"Never mind that," said Hermes. "Wait until they see how fast I can run!"

"They won't care about that once they see how strong I am!" boasted Ares.

Poseidon remained quiet, but Athena looked very concerned.

"Um, I don't think that's what Poseidon has in mind," she said.

Hermes saw Poseidon frown. "Well, at least *one* of you has some sense!" Poseidon boomed. "You cannot let the humans find out who you really are. The time for you to make an impact on their lives will come, but to reveal yourself now would mean banishment from Eureka and exile from *ever* ruling on Mount Olympus. Have I made myself clear?"

Artemis, the great archer, looked at Athena and nodded. She put her bow down beside her.

*It's going to be really hard for me to* not *show off my power!* Hermes thought.

"Don't worry, brother, we won't let you down," said Zeus.

"Good," said Poseidon. "Because we have arrived."

The carriage descended through the clouds. Soon, the Greek countryside came into view.

9

"Wow!" said Aphrodite, Goddess of Beauty and Nature. "I bet they grow some beautiful flowers down there. I can't wait to see them!"

This drew a stern look from Poseidon.

"Without drawing any attention to myself, of course," Aphrodite added quickly, as the carriage approached the ground.

# CHAPTER 2

# THE CITY OF ARGOS

The young gods landed in a wooded area just outside of the small city of Argos. They climbed out of the carriage.

Before they left Eureka, Poseidon had asked each of the young Olympians to change out of their long, flowing, godly robes. Those would have attracted too much attention. Instead, they now wore clothing similar to those of the mortals of Argos—tunics, skirts, shirts made of sewn cloths and animal skins, and leather sandals.

Apollo had grumbled when he first saw the shabby-looking outfits. Artemis had rolled her eyes at the skirt she was given. But they both knew better than to question Poseidon.

And so, dressed as humans, the young gods, with Poseidon acting as their chaperone, entered the city and walked among a large crowd of people.

"I never knew there were so many humans!" said Artemis in awe.

"Many humans live in large groups like this," Aphrodite explained.

"That is correct," Poseidon said. "Their numbers help keep them safe from attack. Living in groups also allows humans to benefit from what is produced by others without having to travel long distances to acquire things."

"What kind of things do they produce?" asked Apollo.

"Look for yourselves," said Poseidon, pointing to a sprawling outdoor market just ahead.

"Wow!" said Artemis. "I've never seen so much stuff all in one place!"

The group walked into the loud, busy market. Hermes's eyes opened wide. He saw everything from huge baskets overflowing with fruits and vegetables, to herds of cattle and oxen. He watched as flocks of chickens crossed the busy main path that led right through the middle.

"This is amazing!" he said, strolling through the market.

Hermes saw a table covered with beautiful pottery. Nearby stood a display of bronze sculptures right next to the sculptor, who was busy shaping her next creation with sharp, metal tools. Another table was filled with leather goods, like sandals, clothing, and bags.

And people, everywhere people— talking, yelling, laughing, and haggling over prices.

*So many people!* Hermes thought.

Zeus stepped up to a spice stand filled with wooden bowls, each one holding a different spice. He sniffed at one particularly fragrant bowl. Suddenly, a powerful sneeze erupted from his nose.

*"AAAAA-CHOOOOO!!"*

As the sneeze exploded, thunder
rumbled and lightning flashed across an
otherwise brilliant sunny sky. The spice
vendor looked at Zeus warily, then looked
up at the sky, which was clear once more.

# CHAPTER 3

# WHISPERS IN THE MARKETPLACE

Hermes felt his stomach tighten. *Is this field trip about to end before it even starts?* he wondered nervously. *Are they going to find out that Zeus is a god?*

The spice vendor looked right at Zeus.

"Did *you* make that happen?" he asked. "How can it thunder and lightning on a perfectly clear, sunny day?"

Hermes saw Zeus's face fill with panic. Zeus then glanced at Athena and he seemed to grow calm and focused. A big, dark cloud suddenly formed overhead.

"Maybe it's not as clear as you think," Zeus said, pointing to the cloud he had obviously just created.

The spice vendor looked up, then scratched his head.

"Maybe not," he said, turning to speak with a customer.

Zeus sighed with relief.

"Well done," Poseidon whispered. "That was close, but quick thinking, Zeus."

The little gods continued to move through the market. Their path was suddenly blocked by a huge ox. A clearly frustrated farmer tugged on a rope tied to the ox, trying to move it. A crowd of people started to build up. Carts full of products intended for sale at the market were stuck. The people gathered started to get rowdy.

"Will you get that beast out of our way?!" shouted one man.

"If you can't control your ox, don't bring it to the marketplace!" yelled another. "Some of us need to make a living!"

Reacting instinctively, Ares sprung into action. He lifted the ox and carried it to the other side of the path, clearing the way for everyone to pass.

Hermes stared at Ares in shock. And he was not the only one. Poseidon's face was pale.

*This whole journey is about to end very badly,* Hermes thought.

Athena quickly stepped in front of Ares.

"My friend here grew up working with livestock," she explained. "He has a very fine touch and has learned how to coax even the most stubborn beast into moving."

"But . . . he lifted the ox off the ground!" said one woman. "No mortal can do that—not even the strongest wrestlers in Athens!"

"Ah, that's the beauty of my friend's technique," Athena said, doing what she did best—thinking on her feet, using her great power of wisdom. "It works so well that it just *looks* like the ox is off the ground, but of course, as you pointed out, that's impossible."

Athena hurried Ares and the other young gods away before any more questions could be asked. Hermes looked back over his shoulder and saw the market resume its noisy business.

"We have all got to be more careful," Athena said.

As he moved through the market, Hermes saw two young kids playing next to a pottery stand. They ran and chased each other, laughing. One of the kids accidentally bumped into the stand, causing a large vase to topple from the top shelf.

Reacting instinctively, Hermes dashed to the stand, caught the vase, put it back onto the shelf, and zoomed back to his friends.

The potter, kids, and customers looked back and forth from the shelf to the ground. To them, it must have looked like the vase simply began to fall, then reversed direction as it headed for the ground and put itself back up on the shelf.

"You kids better be more careful when you play!" said the potter, looking baffled but relieved.

"I think *you* should take that advice as well, Hermes!" grumbled Poseidon. "Save your power until you can put it toward something genuinely useful!"

Hermes frowned. *Well, I'm sure the potter thought me saving his vase was useful, even if he didn't know I was the one who did it!*

A short time later as their friends visited other parts of the market, Zeus, Hermes, Aphrodite, and Athena stopped for a picnic lunch in a wooded area away from the town. As they ate, nestled in a grove of trees, they overheard two men whispering a short distance away.

"So it's all set," whispered one man. "I'll make sure the main gate to Argos is left open tonight, just before sunset."

"Perfect," answered the other, looking around to make sure no one could hear them. "The army from Sparta will invade through the open gate once the sun is completely set. By morning, the city of Argos will belong to Sparta!"

The young gods nearby were stunned.

"Argos is going to be attacked tonight!" said Hermes. "We have to do something! We have to stop them!"

"Maybe we should tell the people of Argos," suggested Aphrodite.

"I'm afraid that would just create panic," replied Athena. "They know that they would not be able to defend themselves from an invading army."

"I could stop them with my lightning!" suggested Zeus, completely forgetting how close he had already come to revealing his powers.

"No," said Athena. "I have a better idea."

## THE JOURNEY OF HERMES BEGINS

# CHAPTER 4

"No matter what, we must still keep the fact that we are gods a secret from the mortals," Athena explained.

"So we can't help them?" Zeus asked.

"Not directly, but we can help them help themselves," Athena replied.

"And how do we do that?" asked Aphrodite.

"The largest city in Greece is Athens," explained Athena. "And that is where the main army of Greek soldiers are. They are charged with keeping peace throughout Greece. Hermes, you must use your great speed to run to Athens and warn them that the Spartans are going to invade Argos tonight. You have to convince the soldiers to hurry back to Argos to defend the town."

"Is there enough time before sunset?" Hermes worried.

"Time is short," said Athena. "Which is why you, Hermes, are the only one who can get there quickly enough so the troops have enough time to get back here."

Poseidon's words echoed in Hermes's mind: *Save your power until you can put it toward something genuinely useful!* This, he realized, was the perfect opportunity to do exactly that.

"Okay," he said. "I'll get those soldiers back here, whatever it takes."

"We'll gather the others and do our best to secure all the gates to the city while you are gone," said Athena.

Hermes nodded, then he turned to Zeus. "Do *you* have any advice for me?" Hermes asked.

"Yes," said Zeus. "Run very, very fast."

Hermes laughed, then he dashed away from Argos.

*This feels like the most important thing I have ever done,* Hermes thought as he sped along the rough dirt road leading to Athens. He rushed past farms and forests. *I know I like to joke around, but this mission will prove that I can be serious when it comes to using my powers and helping mortals.*

After a short while, Hermes arrived at a wide, rushing river. Standing at the edge and catching his breath, he saw the road continue on the other side.

*How am I going to get across?*

He looked left and right, but there seemed to be no bridge or rock formation that would allow him to cross easily.

Then he got an idea.

*This might be crazy, but I think I can run fast enough to skim across the water's surface and make it to the other side before I sink. I've got to try it. Everyone's depending on me. I can't let them down.*

Hermes backed up, then started running as fast as his legs would take him. Leaping off the shoreline, he splashed into the river, his legs pumping. At first, his plan seemed to be working.

*I'm staying on top of the water!*

He pushed his legs to go even faster. But after skimming the surface for a few yards, he felt himself sinking.

*No!* he thought, as the water came up to his waist. Then the mighty river dragged him under.

Pumping his arms and legs while holding his breath, Hermes was swept away by the raging current. *Not only might I fail this mission, but I might not even survive!*

# THE GATHERING STORM

Thrashing underwater, feeling his breath starting to run out, Hermes's thoughts turned to his friends, his mentors, and his mission. Poseidon's voice again echoed in his head:

*Save your power until you can put it toward something genuinely useful!*

Then another voice entered his mind. It was the voice of Athena, who had become a good friend to Hermes. He recalled advice she had given to Zeus during the young gods' first days at Eureka:

*Slow down. Breathe. Focus. Your power is an extension of who you are.*

Hermes calmed his mind. He stopped fighting the current and focused on the strength in his arms and legs. With a powerful thrust, he shot himself back up to the surface.

Filling his lungs with air, Hermes took powerful strokes and swam to the far shore. He crawled out onto the grass, flopped onto his back, and took several deep breaths.

"Well, I made it across the river," he said to himself. "Athena was right. I've got to use my brain along with my legs."

"But right now, I need my legs to get me back on the right path," he said dashing off, following the shoreline back to the main route.

Turning back onto the road, Hermes cranked up all the speed he could muster. *I've lost precious minutes with my blunder at the river,* he thought. *Now, I've got to make up time.*

As he ran, Hermes noticed the sky begin to darken. *Wait! I didn't lose that much time at the river! It can't already be sunset.*

The sun broke through a thick, gray cloud. It was still high in the sky.

*Ok, it's not sunset. It's just a cloud*, he thought.

But a few minutes later, Hermes realized that this was more than just a passing cloud. The sky darkened and the wind picked up. Big gusts blew into Hermes's face and chest, pushing back against his best efforts to run.

*This is the last thing I need now when I'm trying to make up time!*

Then the rain started, just a drizzle at first, but quickly picking up in intensity. Thick, heavy drops of rain started splattering on Hermes's head. Within a few minutes, the fat raindrops turned into blinding sheets of water pummeling Hermes from above. The fierce wind combined with the sudden downpour to slam a wall of water into Hermes's face. Thunder boomed and lightning flashed.

"I can hardly see where I'm going!" Hermes shouted, struggling to move forward and power his way through the relentless forces of nature. "I could sure use Zeus's help right about now to get rid of this storm!"

Suddenly, something big and black appeared in front of him, as if a wall had appeared from out of nowhere. Skidding to a stop and trying to keep his footing on the slick, muddy path, Hermes crashed into the big black wall in front of him. He tumbled to the ground.

Then the wall started moving toward him!

# HERMES, THE SHEPHERD?

"Help!" cried a thin, strained voice, drifting out from somewhere in the water and wind.

Hermes leapt to his feet and bumped into the side of a huge black cow—the "wall" that had sprung up in front of him. Behind that cow was another, followed by some sheep, all panicked and hurrying across the road, blocking Hermes's path.

Squeezing between the cows and sheep, Hermes came upon an old shepherd who was frantically trying to herd the animals back toward his farm.

"I had just opened the gate to go in and make sure the livestock had enough food when the storm hit suddenly," the shepherd shouted to be heard over the sound of the pounding rain. "They got spooked and ran out, and now I can't get them back into their fenced area. Can you help me, young stranger?"

Hermes was not sure what to do. He wanted to help, but he was running out of time. He wished that Poseidon or Athena were here to help him decide.

But looking at the road ahead, he realized that even if he wanted to continue on his journey, he couldn't. The road was now totally blocked by the herd.

"I will help you," Hermes shouted to the shepherd. "You head back to the gate. I'll drive the herd toward you."

The shepherd nodded. "Thank you for your kindness, young stranger!" Then he ran off toward the fenced-in area.

Sloshing through the soupy rain and battling against the whipping wind, Hermes ran alongside the herd. When he reached the front and was certain that the shepherd couldn't see him, he started running back and forth at blinding speed, creating a one-man wall. He slowly changed direction and started guiding the herd back around toward their pasture.

Hermes ran behind the animals shouting, "Ya! Ya!" The herd picked up speed, and was now running in the right direction.

The rain started to slow down, the wind eased, and the skies began to brighten just as the first animals reached the shepherd's grounds. With the storm passing, the old man easily herded the cows and sheep through the open gate. When the last animal was safely behind the fence, the shepherd closed and latched the gate.

"Well done, young stranger," said the shepherd. "I think you would make a fine shepherd."

Hermes smiled. "I'll keep that in mind," he said.

"And thank you again," said the shepherd. "May I repay you for your kind deed by making you a hot meal? I make really good eggs! It is the least I could do."

At the mention of food, Hermes's stomach grumbled. He had burned so much energy running at top speed, getting across the river, and herding the flock that he was now very hungry. A hot meal sounded great to him. Then he pictured himself trying to explain to Poseidon and the others that he was too late to save Argos because he had stopped to eat.

"Thank you, but I'm in a rush today. Maybe another time," he said.

Hermes resumed his journey along the path toward Athens.

*Between the river, the storm, and the herd, I've lost so much time!*

Another hour passed. Hermes rounded a bend in the road, and there, looming just ahead like a magical kingdom out of a fairy tale, was Athens, rising out of the plains. He saw the white marble of the Parthenon gleaming in the sunshine.

"There it is!" Hermes shouted, instantly re-energized. "I'm almost there. Now, to complete my journey!"

But just as Hermes took his next step, a huge creature leaped out from behind a nearby boulder, landing right in the middle of the road, blocking his path. The enormous beast was unlike anything Hermes had ever seen. It had the body of a lion and the head of a woman.

"You cannot pass!" the creature announced, slamming a huge paw filled with razor-sharp claws into the ground just inches away from Hermes.

# CHAPTER 7
# RIDDLES OF THE SPHINX

"Who—I mean *what*—I mean *who* are you?" Hermes stammered, trying to make sense of the strange creature before him.

"I am known as the Sphinx," said the creature in what to Hermes was a surprisingly human-sounding voice. "None may pass to enter the city of Athens unless they solve my riddles."

"I DON'T HAVE TIME FOR GAMES!" he shouted. "I've got a city to save."

Using his great speed, Hermes tried to dash around the Sphinx. To his shock, she moved just as quickly as he did and again stood in his way.

"None may pass to enter the city of Athens unless they solve my riddles."

"Yeah, I heard you the first time," Hermes mumbled. "All right. Give me the first riddle, I guess."

"Very well," said the Sphinx. "What is it that can only be used if it is broken?"

Pacing back and forth, Hermes thought as hard as he could.

*That doesn't make any sense. How can you use something if it's broken? I can't believe I'm going to fail my mission because of a stupid riddle!*

As he paced anxiously, his stomach grumbled loudly.

*I'm sure I could think better if I had something to eat. Anything, an apple, even a couple of . . . those shepherd's eggs. Eggs! That's it!*

"The answer to your first riddle is an egg," Hermes said. "You can only use an egg if it is broken. And I wish I had a couple to break and fry up right—"

"Correct," said the Sphinx, interrupting him. "Here is the second riddle. The more of this there is, the less you are able to see. What is it?"

*Again, that sounds impossible. If there is more of something, how can it be harder to see?*

Hermes glanced up at the sky, growing more worried than ever about reaching Athens and getting the soldiers back to Argos before dark.

*Dark . . . darkness! That's it!*

"The answer to your second riddle is darkness," Hermes said. "The more darkness there is, the less you are able to see."

"Correct," said the Sphinx, narrowing her eyes. "Here is the third riddle. What runs but never walks, has a mouth but never talks, has a head but can't think, and has a bed but does not sleep?"

*Wow! This is harder than the first two.*

Hermes thought about every challenge he'd had to endure to get this far. He felt frustrated that after the storm and the cattle and crossing the raging river, he might fail just because of a—

*Wait a minute . . . the river—that's it!*

"The answer to your third riddle is a river," Hermes said. "It runs and has a mouth, head, and bed."

"Correct," said the Sphinx. "Here is the final riddle. If you answer this correctly, you may pass along this road to Athens. The more of these you take, the more of these you leave behind. What are they?"

Hermes thought for a few minutes but found himself no closer to a solution.

*I don't know! I just don't know!*

# CHAPTER 8

# ATHENS, AT LAST

Frantic, and now certain that he would fail his mission, Hermes paced back and forth across the road. The Sphinx watched him, smirking. Looking down dejectedly, Hermes saw the footprints he had made during his pacing. Then he glanced back at the long path of footprints he made on his journey along the road.

And that's when it came to him.

"Footsteps!" he shouted. "The answer is footsteps. The more you take, the more you leave behind."

"Correct," said the Sphinx, looking a little disappointed. "You . . . may pass."

The Sphinx bounded away from the path. Within seconds, she had disappeared from sight.

"Now to complete my mission," said Hermes, taking off down the path.

Athens grew larger with every step.

As Hermes entered the city, he was stunned by how much bigger it was than Argos. He quickly raced through the city, searching for someone to help him. Hermes saw long rows of houses, great amphitheaters where plays and music were being performed, and huge stadiums where athletes competed and crowds cheered. And, unlike Argos, there was not one market, but at least five—all filled with crops and livestock and more people than Hermes could have ever imagined.

At one of these markets, Hermes spotted two soldiers. He hurried over to them.

"Argos needs your help!" Hermes blurted out. "They are going to be attacked tonight at sunset. They need soldiers to defend the city."

The soldiers looked at each other skeptically.

"Who are you?" one soldier asked. "And how do you know this?"

"I overheard the plot," Hermes replied. "Please, Argos needs your help now!"

"Our captain is right over there," said one of the soldiers, pointing. "You have to talk with him."

Hermes hurried over to the captain and told him of the plot.

The captain looked at Hermes suspiciously. "You say you overheard this yourself?" the captain asked. "Where, here in Athens?"

"No, I overheard it in Argos this very morning," Hermes said.

"*This* morning?" the captain asked, looking around. "Well, where's your horse, your carriage?"

"I don't have a horse or carriage," Hermes said, starting to grow impatient and wondering again if everything he had done was for nothing.

"Well then, how did you get from Argos to Athens so quickly?" the captain asked.

"I ran the whole way," Hermes said proudly.

"Impossible!" said the captain. "No one can run that fast."

*How do I make him believe me without revealing my power? I have a chance to help the humans right now. This is what all my training is focused on. And I'm not going to risk lives by waiting.*

"I can run that fast," Hermes said. "Watch this."

With the captain and the other two soldiers looking on in amazement, Hermes sped through the market. He ran from table to table, stopping at every vendor in the market before returning to the captain's side in a matter of seconds with a handful of food.

The captain stared at him. "You know, if you weren't a kid, I'd almost think you were one of the gods. With your great speed, you should consider competing in the games here in Athens—when you are a bit older."

"So, will you help the people of Argos?" Hermes asked, taking a bite out of an apple he had bought at one of the vendors.

The captain thought for a moment, then said, "We shall!" Then he turned to the two soldiers. "Round up the rest of the garrison and prepare our horses and carriages. We ride for Argos!"

"Thank you!" said Hermes.

He sped back out of Athens, pausing to get one last pie from a vendor before he left.

Stuffing the pie into his mouth as he ran, Hermes glanced up and saw the sun starting to make its way lower in the sky.

I only hope I'm not too late!

## CHAPTER 9

# THE RETURN TO ARGOS

Hermes sped along the road back to Argos.

*I've got to get back and let my friends know that the Greek army is on their way.*

He saw something ahead blocking the path. As he got closer, Hermes realized that it was the Sphinx.

*Oh no, not again!*

Hermes saw a family of travelers heading toward Athens who had been stopped by the Sphinx.

A man, a woman, and two young children all paced anxiously in front of the Sphinx. As Hermes approached, he overheard them.

"I can't believe that we answered her first three riddles, but that this last one will prevent us from reaching Athens," said the man. "This whole long journey will have been for naught."

78

"I've looked at it from all angles, but I still can't figure it out," said the woman. "*The more of these you take, the more of these you leave behind. What are they? What can the answer be?*"

Reaching the back of the Sphinx, Hermes scooted around her. She made no move to stop him.

*I guess only travelers heading toward Athens have to answer riddles, not those traveling away from the city.*

As he passed the family, Hermes slowed down and shouted, "Footsteps! The answer is footsteps!"

"Footsteps!" cried the woman. "Of course. Thank you, kind traveler!"

"Hey, that's not fair!" the Sphinx cried.

Speeding away, Hermes glanced back over his shoulder and saw the Sphinx reluctantly getting out of the way so the family could pass. The Sphinx caught Hermes's eye and sneered at him, making him hope he wouldn't have to pass this way again anytime soon.

A few minutes later, Hermes spotted a man standing in the road waving his arms. *What now?* Hermes wondered.

As he got closer, he recognized the man as the shepherd he had helped on his way to Athens. The old man waved him over and Hermes slowed to stop.

"How's the herd?" Hermes asked.

"Everyone is where they should be, thanks to you, my young friend," replied the shepherd. "Here, I want you to have something I made. I have been working on it for a long time, and I can't think of anyone I'd rather give it to."

The shepherd handed Hermes a tall wooden staff. At the top of the staff sat a beautifully carved pair of wings. "For one whose feet move as swiftly as the wings of a bird," said the shepherd.

Hermes took the staff and held it up. "Thank you. It's beautiful. But now, I must hurry."

"Be off then, young friend, and may the gods guide you," said the shepherd.

Soon, Hermes approached the river that had given him so much trouble earlier.

*When I got carried away by the current, I found a much narrower spot to cross*, he recalled. Turning off the road, he dashed through the woods until he came to the narrow section of the river. Clutching his new staff tightly, he ran across the short span to the other side. A quick jog back through the woods and he returned to the path.

Finally, he spotted Argos just ahead. Glancing up at the sky, Hermes saw the sun start to drop behind the mountains.

# CHAPTER 10

# JOURNEY'S END

Rushing through the gathering dusk, Hermes arrived at the main gate to Argos. Poseidon, Ares, Apollo, and Artemis were there, waiting.

"What took you so long?" Ares asked.

"Yeah, Apollo and I thought we were going to have to take on the whole Spartan army by ourselves," said Artemis.

"This is not the time for jokes," said Poseidon. "Hermes, were you successful?"

"Yes, though I had a heck of a time on that road," replied Hermes. "First, there was this river that—"

"There will be plenty of time for stories later," Poseidon said, interrupting him. "What about the Greek army?"

"They are right behind me, traveling by horseback and carriage, so they should be here soon," Hermes explained.

"How did you convince them to help the town?" Apollo asked.

Thinking it wise not to reveal to Poseidon that he had to use his power to convince the Greek captain to help, Hermes said, "I used my charming personality. Good thing we didn't send you, Apollo." Apollo rolled his eyes in response.

At that moment, the sun disappeared behind the mountain.

"It is time," Poseidon said anxiously.

"Hermes!" came a shout from nearby.

Zeus, Athena, and Aphrodite came running up to the group.

"We've sabotaged the other gates to Argos so they won't open," said Zeus. "We just have this one left."

"Is the army coming?" asked Athena.

Hermes nodded, then asked, "How did you sabotage the gates?"

"Watch," said Zeus. Looking around to make sure that no mortals could see him, Zeus fired a small, controlled lightning bolt at the metal latch on the gate. The metal glowed red, then fused together. "It won't stop them completely, but it will slow them down until help arrives."

"Come, let us get out of sight," said Poseidon.

The gods hurried to a nearby grove of trees. A few seconds later, the invading army of Sparta came marching toward the gate.

"There must be over a hundred soldiers!" Ares whispered.

"Quiet!" Poseidon said tersely.

The Spartan soldiers reached the gate. One soldier yanked on the latch, but it wouldn't budge.

"What?! The gate was supposed to be left open," said another soldier.

"Someone has melted the latch!" cried another. "That means that they knew we were coming!"

"No matter," blustered the Spartan captain. "Argos has no army. We will destroy the latch, open this gate, and take the city."

He pulled out an axe and smashed it into the latch with the flat side. After a few blows, the metal shattered and the main gate to Argos swung open wide.

"There!" shouted the Spartan captain. "What did I tell you? Prepare to enter the—"

He stopped short at the sound of thundering hooves pounding on the road from the direction of Athens. A few seconds later, the Greek army arrived. After a brief skirmish, they pinned the Spartan soldiers against the city's outer walls.

"Wow, there must be five hundred Greek soldiers," Ares said. "You really did it, Hermes!"

Realizing that they were surrounded and vastly outnumbered, the Spartans reluctantly surrendered.

"And if you have any ideas of ever coming back, remember: We are just down the road," said the Greek captain. He watched as the Spartan army marched away in defeat.

Hermes and the others stepped out from their hiding place and greeted the army.

"Thank you, captain," said Hermes.

The captain nodded, then spotted Poseidon. He pointed at Hermes and said, "This boy here, he is quite fast. And brave. You should be proud."

The army marched away, heading back to Athens.

Poseidon shot a glance at Hermes, who looked away. "Come," he announced after a few moments. "Pegasus and his team will be arriving soon in the wooded area where they dropped us off. We must meet them and return to Eureka. I hope you found this experience with mortals educational."

Hermes breathed a sigh of relief. "You bet!" said Hermes, as the young gods started walking toward the woods. "Did you hear the captain? He said I was brave!"

"Oh, we are *never* going to hear the end of this," said Apollo.

"You wouldn't believe what I had to go through," said Hermes. "First, there was this rushing river I had to cross. Oh, and I met this weird creature that was half lion and half woman."

Even the usually patient Athena rolled her eyes. But Hermes continued.

"And I saved a shepherd's flock during a terrible storm. In fact, he was so grateful, he gave me this." Hermes held up his staff. "At first, he offered to cook me a meal, but—"

Hermes felt his stomach grumble again at the mention of food.

"And speaking of a meal, all that running has left me starving. Does anyone have any food?"

# Look for more books by these creators...

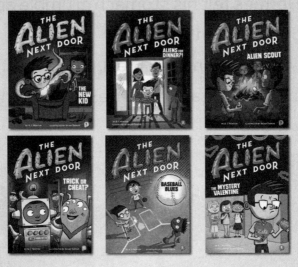

...and read on for a sneak peek at the fourth book in the Little Olympians series

BOOK 4

# Little Olympians

## ARTEMIS, THE ARCHER GODDESS

CHAPTER 1

# BIG NEWS!

Artemis and Athena stared at the game in front of them. They were concentrating hard as they played petteia, a very complicated board game. Athena was the current petteia champion at Camp Eureka.

Artemis really wanted to beat her.

Poseidon, their mentor and counselor at Eureka, where the young gods were learning to use their great powers, had given his students some time off. They were enjoying a bit of relaxation following their recent intense studies, travels, and adventures.

Artemis and Athena sat on stone seats and leaned over the petteia board. A group of their fellow young gods had gathered around to watch them play.

Aphrodite loved analyzing the various strategies needed to win petteia. She leaned over and watched as Artemis focused intently on her next move.

"If you concentrate any harder, I think you're going to stare a hole right through the game board," Aphrodite joked.

Artemis said nothing and continued to study the board.

Nearby, Apollo and Ares leaned over a thick, sawed-off tree trunk. They were arm wrestling, as Zeus and Hermes looked on.

Their arm muscles bulged. Their teeth

clenched as veins began to pop out of their necks. Their fingers started to turn purple. Yet, so far, neither could budge the other's arm.

"I think the object is to actually move the other guy's arm," Hermes said to his two struggling friends.

But Apollo and Ares were working much too hard to reply.

"It's great to have a little time off," Zeus said to Hermes as they watched the mighty contest. "Poseidon has been training us nonstop since we got to Eureka. We've done so much, it's kind of hard to remember it all. I know that my parents are going to want to hear about *everything* that happened."

Hermes smiled a mischievous smile.

"Well, then why don't we tell them!"

Zeus looked confused. "What do you mean?" he asked.

"I think we should start a newspaper," Hermes said, getting very excited by the idea. "We could report on all our accomplishments and everything that happens here. Then we could circulate it around the camp and share it with our families back home, too. I know that my parents would sure be proud of my heroic run that saved the city of Argos!"

"Gotcha!" Ares shouted, finally pinning Apollo's arm to the top of the tree stump.

"No fair!" Apollo complained. "My elbow slipped."

"And who wouldn't want to read about Ares's big arm wrestling win, or Apollo's excuses and whining about losing?" Hermes continued.

At that moment, Artemis and Athena joined the others, having finished their game. "What are you two talking about?"

"I'm going to start a newspaper to cover all the important events here at Eureka," Hermes explained.

"Well, I have your first headline," said Artemis, raising her hands. "Artemis is Camp Eureka's new petteia champion after beating Athena!"

Athena smiled, taking her loss in stride. "Well, that *is* big news," she said.

"That's it!" Hermes cried. "I'll call the newspaper . . . the *Eureka News*. I better get to work on the first issue!"